AF419329

OUTLAWS PUBLISHING

BLACK HORSE SALOON

JOHN THURMOND

For information contact: info@outlawspublishing.com

Cover Art by Michael Thomas
Cover design by Outlaws Publishing
Edited by Ann Mealler
Published by Outlaws Publishing
April 2021
10987654321

Chapter 1

After semi-retiring from US Marshal Service, I, Sam Bass, the only black man ever that was a US Marshal for Indian Territory, still moved prisoners for Judge Isaac Parker from the lockup to the courthouse, but only the dangerous ones. I actually never retired. I just stopped working every day. I still had my badge. Judge Parker knew I would just strap my old double barrel shotgun to the necks of the prisoners and lead them to trial. What kind of idiot would try to escape when you have a shot gun strapped to your neck with a belt run through a ring welded at the end of the sawed off barrels of an old ten gauge shot gun with double hammers and triggers?

I always put on a good show parading an outlaw down the street, and always stopped to talk to the town folks. With both hammers cocked back and my fingers on the triggers, I would just walk the prisoners right on into the court room and sit them down before I removed the belt and my shotgun. And, I always told the judge, "I will be right outside if you need me."

I never counted up the money I "borrowed" for my retirement from the Hollister Bank one night. When I finally got around to it, it kind of scared me some. There was more there than I figured on. The total came to over twenty-five thousand dollars. *'I can't ever spend that kind of money in Fort Smith," he thought. 'Old Judge*

Parker will know where it came from. He's already asked me twice about the robbery and shoot out that night.'

I had already told the judge about me leaving Frederick, Oklahoma after hanging the man he sent me there to hang with Judge Parker's rope. The man was a black farmer and sentenced to hang by the neck until he was dead. Seems after a dance on Saturday night, he killed his wife for flirting with another man. He blamed it on a horse he startled when they were walking home that night, but there weren't no horse tracks where he claimed it happened. The sheriff found a bloody axe handle in his barn, and the judge sentenced him to hang.

With him being the first man to be hanged in the new state of Oklahoma, and not wounding to cause a riot, Judge Parker had sent a black man to get the job done. It just happened to be me and it was the first hanging in the New State of Oklahoma. Judge Parker sent me, a black US Deputy Marshal, to hang the man.

After getting the job done, I left town just before dark, not wanting to spend the night in Frederick, Oklahoma. The man I had just hung probably had a hundred friends in and around town, so I headed east, going back to Fort Sill where I had rented a buggy so I could catch a stage going back to Ft. Smith, Arkansas the next morning.

Realizing I handed eaten since that morning, I was awful hungry. So, I stopped in Hollister, Oklahoma, about twelve miles east of Frederick, for supper. After paying my food bill and leaving at dusk, I could hear gun shots behind me. Turning around and going back, I encountered some men firing at the front windows of the bank. Storming up the sidewalk, hollering "what's going on here," the banker told me he was being robbed. Having my shotgun with me, I just blew out all the windows and front doors and ran into the bank and blew ever thing away I could see, including the back door. I ran outside and shot at some riders going south toward a little town called Loveland. I told the banker I seen them headed southeast and they got away.

"Send for the sheriff over at Frederick. He can track them down in the morning. I needed to get back to Ft. Smith, Arkansas with the judge's hanging rope. If I'm late, he will have my hide tanned," I told the banker, then left town.

Now, that's the story I told Judge Parker. What really happened was, after eating my supper in the Hollister Café and hearing the banker tell the owner of the café, "If I ever see you serve a black man in here again, I will call your bank note and you can either pay up or leave town yourself," I got kind of upset.

Not wanting to cause any trouble, I paid for my meal and left town. I pulled my buggy around behind the bank and forced the back door in just as the sun went down. All the while I was thinking, *'Well, Mr. Banker, I will just call your note in myself and clean you out.'*

I cleaned out the safe (that wasn't locked) and was fixing to leave when the first shots rang out. The banker and his teller were standing across the street and seen a flash of light as I came in the back door. It faced west into the setting sun. The sun had just gone down and it was dark inside. The only light was the flash of the guns being fired at me from across the street. There was on old gun in the safe and a box of shells. I grabbed it and fired back at them until I was out of shells. I just threw the old gun back into the safe and left out the back door.

There was not a person around, just me and my buggy, so I headed north toward Fort Sill. About a mile north of town, I could still hear them shooting into the bank, so I turned around and drove back. I put on a white duster that came with the rented buggy I had and filled a pocket full of shotgun shells. I jumped out of the buggy, and making all the noise I could, stomped up the boardwalk and helped them run the 'outlaws' out of the bank. There wasn't much of the place left after a pocket full of ten gauge double ought buck shot. All the windows and doors were gone, and all the desks were shot up. The back door was shot out, too. There were enough footprints around the back so that you could not tell if there was one person or a hundred that robbed the bank.

Later on, I got worried about the money and built me a double floor in the back of my buggy. I laid all them bills out flat and covered them with another floor and nailed it down, just take it with me wherever I went. I figured that way, if Judge Parker ever came looking for me and I wasn't home, he might accidently find it and I would be the one hanging from his gallows. So, I kept the money hid in my buggy.

It was colder than hell that winter. I spent a lot of my daytime at Relies Bar, playing cards. It just nickel and dime poker, a lot of times it was just a penny. I was just passing time. I got to talking with a whiskey salesman named Hiram Jones, who worked for a whiskey maker from Kentucky. He was always talking about how much money there was to be made in the bar business and talked about opening up his own saloon someday. I told him if I ever had one, it would be a long ways south of here where it never got cold. I was damned tired of being cold all the time, especially after getting older.

I told Hiram one day about being a US Marshal for Isaac Parker, but I never worked much anymore. I was getting too old to ride a horse all day, let alone for a month or more. Besides, I kind of liked my buggy because it had one of them horsehair stuffed seats and a surrey top I could let up or down.

Hiram said, "you might like some of the things I've collected over the years."

"What's that?" I asked.

Hiram opened up his carpet bag, the one he kept whiskey samples in, and pulled out several handguns. He laid them out on the tabletop one at a time, telling me which ones had belonged to outlaws. The first one he laid out was a nickel-plated Russian .44 short rim fire. He said it was the gun that killed Jessie James. Well, I knew that was a lie, but I never told him. I just let him talk.

Hiram finally pulled out an old Colt .45 with no bluing left and pearl handle grips. He said, "I got this one off a sheriff up at Coffeeville, Missouri for a dollar. It has a lot of wear. The sheriff said there wasn't much telling how many men this old gun killed. Maybe none, but the sheriff said he was sure it came off the outlaw trail."

I took my cards and turned the old gun over and seen the scar on the barrel. Trying to keep calm, I asked Hiram what he would take for the old Colt.

"Heck, Sam, if you want it, give me two dollars and it's yours."

I paid Hiram his two dollars and checked the gun for shells. It was empty. I shoved it in my pocket, stayed a while and went home close to dark. I sat in my rocker in front of the fireplace and went to sleep holding the old Colt in my lap. It was the same one I had carried all the time I was a US Marshal and the same gun Marie La Veau, the Voodoo Queen in New Orleans, had warned me about being an evil gun.

I had carried that Colt all the time I rode all over Indian territory. It saved my life several times and killed a lot of men. I had given it to a lifelong friend, a man named Bob Ford. I knew it was the gun that killed Jesse James. I had warned Bob Ford not to point it at anyone he did not intend to kill. I also warned Bob not to point the gun at just at anyone. When they carried Bob to trial, he swore he just pointed the gun at Jesse and it went off by accident, killing him. Now, the gun had come back to me. I pondered on just why before I went to sleep.

I had a dream that night about a woman I met one time in New Orleans. She was a voodoo queen buy the name of Marie La Veau. She was the one that told me the gun I carried was an evil gun because it had been struck by lightning. She said it would kill anyone I pointed it at, good or bad, and I needed to be very careful who I pointed it at. She warned that they will be killed and that the evil of the gun would consume me if I let it.

Marie was a fine looking woman. She had on a red dress and a white shawl wrapped around her shoulders. Her long silky hair was adorned with bird feathers tied in it; some red and green ones. She had big dark eyes and smooth light brown skin. I was thinking she was the prettiest woman I ever laid eyes on. She just seemed to float around my room and talked all the time. She told me to give the old Colt to a Texas Ranger, the one that knows the law she said, and disappeared from my dream. I woke up when the gun slipped out of my hand and landed on the floor.

Walking back from the outhouse, the sun was just coming up. I kept thinking about what Marie told me. The Texas Ranger that knows the law she said. Now, who would she be talking about I wondered?

Things just started to happen that day before I reached my porch. My next door neighbor hollered at me.

"Sam, can I talk to you a minute? My oldest boy is getting married to a girl from the Nations and I would like for them to live close to his mother and not move away. Would you be interested in an offer for your house and barn?"

I scratched my head and said, "Well, I been thinking about warmer winters south of here a ways. How much do you think my old place is worth?"

"Sam," my neighbor said, "I can offer you a thousand dollars cash money and that's about all I can afford."

I told him to send his son over at noon and we'd make out a deed for the place and get it recorded at the county courthouse.

As soon as it was done, I went to the hardware and bought traveling supplies, along with a belt and holster for the old Colt and shells. The next sunrise found me in my buggy with my old saddle horse tied on the back. The buggy was loaded up with all I owned and I was headed south to warmer weather. I never turned in my US Marshal badge. In fact, I still had it pinned on my shirt, thinking I might have need of it because the road I was taking south to Fort Worth, Texas went through the Indian Nations. It was now called Oklahoma, but I knew it was still wild country.

Chapter 2

I paid my dime for the ferry boat ride across the Arkansas River for the last time and headed south west. I made it to McAlester before dark and knew of a place that would let me a room for the night. I also knew the livery man would let me keep my buggy inside the livery barn in case it rained. I liked to keep my seat dry.

It was raining the next morning when I made my way to the café. It looked like it would drizzle all day and I wasn't in any hurry. I stayed two days in McAlester before it cleared up, but it was still cloudy when I finally left and headed southwest down a trail I knew would take me to Fort Worth, Texas.

The Red River was high when I found it two days later. It was kind of narrow with fast water, but I knew the river got wider on farther west of where I was at. So, I just headed west until I came to a wider place with more shallow water and a lot of red sand. I mounted my saddle horse and tied the lead rope to the buggy horse. I crossed the Red River and headed on south. The first town I came to was Decatur, Texas. I had no hankering to go farther west to Denton, Texas, where I was raised, so I just headed on south.

I had to spend the night in the livery barn and cleaned up in a horse tank. The sun found me sitting on the steps of the sheriff's office. An old white haired man by the name of John McKenzie told me he was the sheriff. I told him who I was and that I was a US Marshal out of Fort Smith, Arkansas.

"What can I do for you?" John asked.

"We need to visit a spell about Texas Rangers," I told him. "It may take a while."

"Well, let's go eat and talk," said John.

I found a table in the back of the café' next to the Longhorn Saloon. The waiter was about to tell me to leave when John came in and sat down with me. I showed my badge.

After having bacon and eggs and over coffee, I asked John, "If I asked you which Texas Ranger knows the law, what name would you give me?"

"What are you talking about, Sam?"

I told John about the voodoo queen, Marie La Veau, and the dream I had where she was floating around the room telling me to give the item I had to the Texas Ranger who knows the law.

"I've heard about her," John said. "Scary as hell, I've been told, but a real good looking woman."

"Yeah," I said. "I met her one time down in New Orleans and I ain't got over her yet. I know what to give this Ranger, I just don't know who he is."

"What is the item she wants you to give to this Ranger who knows the law?" John asked.

I pulled the Colt out and laid it on the table. I told John palm the gun, but not to point it at any one and don't drop it. "You're in for a surprise. Be careful."

John picked up the Colt and got the shock of his life. He almost dropped it before he laid it back on the table. "What the heck?" John said.

I told John what Marie told me the first time we met down in New Orleans; about the gun being evil. "It will kill any one you point it at. The gun makes anyone who picks it up its owner and it will protect you from harm. It just kills anyone trying to kill you and it don't care who they are. I carried this gun all the time I was in the Nations. I got into a lot of gun fights and never missed a shot and it saved my life every time. It just seems to jump into your hand when its needed. Scared the heck out of me several times, but Marie told me to give it to a Texas Ranger, the one that knows the law. That's all she said."

John sat there for close to an hour, drinking coffee. Finally, he said, "I know who she was talking about. He's a young smart aleck Texas Ranger who knew more about Texas Law than anyone else. Rangers got him teaching a law class down at Waco, a place called Baylor, I believe. A man by the name of Beacher Tolbert. When you get to Waco, see the sheriff, a man named Mack Boyles. He can tell you how to find Beacher Tolbert."

"Yeah, I met Mack Boyles," I told John. "Matter of fact, he's the one gave that me this old Colt a longtime ago."

I had been there before, when I was a young man running away from my adopted home and worked for the stockyards loading box cars for a dollar a day. I knew where Waco was.

I wasn't in any hurry. It took two days getting to Waco. I got the livery man to put up my horses and buggy and found the old hotel that used to let me a room. The next morning after cleaning up, I met Mack Boyles; same old sheriff, just a little older.

I nearly forgot my given name was John Harris and not Sam Bass. Mack recognized me right off. After visiting a spell, I told him I was a US Marshal out of Fort Smith and had to change my name because of a little incident on the Mississippi River, south of Memphis. "No big deal, but I changed it to Sam Bass when Judge Parker hired me on as a US Marshal, I told him. "There's a little thing down here in Texas I need to take care of. I need to give something to a Texas Ranger by the name of Beacher Tolbert. You got any idea where I can find him?"

Mack sat there a spell and finally said, "I believe he's down at Del Rio with two other Rangers, chasing a Mexican bandito by the name of Poncho Villa. That's about two hundred miles southwest of here, maybe farther. I've never been there myself, but I will tell you right now, get you a barrel of water, maybe two, if you got a buggy because it's a long, dry trip I've heard tell."

I got myself two barrels, along with camp supplies and a map, before I left Waco. I also bought a new Winchester rifle in .44/40 and a new Colt pistol of the same caliber. I still carried the older Colt, just in case. *'You never know what or who you might run into,'* I thought. *'I might meet some of them Mescalero Apache Indians. Never seen one, but I might get the chance, and I'd hate to get shot at and not be able to shoot back.'*

I picked up an old dog on the trail. *'Heck,'* I thought, *'we're fifty miles from the nearest homestead. Where did he come from?'* The dog was just barely able to walk. He did not look that old, just tired from walking. He either got lost or lost his owner to the Indians. Either way, he needed some help, so I stopped and gave him some water and dried beef from my supplies. I loaded him up in the back of my buggy. He just laid down and went to sleep.

I camped that night in a gully and had a small fire going. After dark, the old dog jumped out of the buggy and caught himself a rabbit. He brought it back to camp and had himself a meal. The only thing he wanted from me was a drink of water.

'I think I'll call him John,' I thought, and had myself a good laugh over that. The dog did not seem to care. At least I would have someone to talk to. It was a long way to Del Rio, Texas.

I covered my fire with sand and left my coffee pot setting on top so it would still be warm in the morning. I spread some ashes around my blanket to keep the scorpions and snakes away, rolled up in my tarp and went to sleep.

Old John woke me up with a whimper and I saw him crawling off towards the sage brush like he was sneaking up on a rabbit. For some reason, I rolled out of my tarp and under my buggy and watched that old dog. He was sneaking up on an Indian who was about to shoot an arrow into my bed tarp. I still had my gun on. I just pulled it out and emptied it into the sage brush. I stayed up the rest of the night drinking coffee.

Come daybreak, I found an old Indian with several scalps under his belt, dead. I looked around for other tracks, but found none. Apparently, he was alone and on foot. Old John was happy when we broke camp. He just took a whiz on the dead Indian and we left him there, face up in the morning sun. If I was right, I was still three or four days from Del Rio.

I came to a crossroad sign late that evening that said Uvalde south, Del Rio west. Now that I thought about it, Mack said Beacher could be in either Uvalde or Del Rio. Uvalde looked to be closer on my map, so I headed to Uvalde.

I got there late the next day and found a livery stable and a cantina. Old John was happy to stay with the buggy. I left him some water and dried beef and made my way to the cantina for beans and steak. There were a lot of Mexicans around, some a lot darker than I was. No one paid me any mind. I got what I wanted to eat and a cool beer. After dinner, I heard some shots and saw a lot of Mexican banditos in town. A man I was talking to said they all wear them banderillos around their necks to carry extra bullets in. I counted ten in a group. They were talking about some Texas Rangers and they were tired of being chased. Looked like I got here just in time, if one of them was Beacher Tolbert. The banditos said they were just going to shoot him on sight. The bandits all left town at dark and back across the border to Ciudad Acuna, Mexico.

I decided I needed to look the sheriff up found him sitting in his office looking at wanted posters. I showed him my badge told him who I was. His name was Roho Gonzales. I asked him if he knew a Ranger Tolbert.

"Which one?" Roho asked. "Luke or Beacher?"

"Beacher's the one I'm looking for," I told him. "I never met either one of them, but I've got something I need to give Beacher."

"How fast you need to find Beacher?" Roho asked.

"Well, from the looks of things, right now if I could."

Roho sat there a spell and told me to cross the river and ride to Ciudad Acuna, about a half mile south of the Rio. "Find Rosa's Cantina," he said. "All three Rangers are there nearly every night. The tall leather tanned one is Hitch Westmoreland and the short red-headed one is Red O'Fallon. The other one is Beacher Tolbert. He has big arms, narrow waist, medium height and sandy hair. He only wears one gun, right handed."

I thanked Roho and left, taking my saddle horse, and rode to Ciudad Acuna, Mexico.

Chapter 3

Ciudad Acuna, Mexico was not a very big place; just a couple of buildings and a dozen adobes, all flat top small homes. Some had walls made of mud around them and just tall enough to keep in the pigs and chickens. I found the cantina Roho had told me about. The whole thing was open to the boardwalk with no hitching rail in front. It was across the street, under a big live oak tree where I tied up my horse up at a water trough and made my way to the boardwalk.

I stood next to a post holding the porch up for a spell, watching people until I found who I was looking for. With oil lamps on every post, the tables inside the cantina were well lit. All three Rangers were having a meal and there was an empty chair at their table. I eased over there and stood until they all looked up at me. I just opened my lapel and showed them my US Marshal badge. Beacher shoved the extra chair out with his foot and I sat down, waved the girl over and ordered the same thing they were having.

"Filetey juevos," I told the girl (steak and eggs). We never said a word until the meal was over.

Finally, Beacher asked me my name. I stuck my hand out and said, "Sam Bass."

Beacher took hold and held on. He said, "I heard about you from one of my kin folks, Joe Tolbert. He said he met you one time up in the Indian Nations. Told me you scared the heck out of him. I kind of wondered why, until now. I understand what he meant now that I've met you."

"Can me and you talk alone?" I asked Beacher. Red and Hitch just got up, walked to the bar and left us alone. I changed chairs and moved over next to Beacher and began to tell him the story about the old Colt revolver with pearl grips. I laid it on the table and told him about Marie La Veau coming to me in a dream. I spent close to an hour getting it all told.

Beacher said, "Well, I never much believed in them voodoo tales myself.

"Well, believe it or not," I told him, "you will after you pick up that old Colt." With that said, I just shoved the old Colt across the table to Beacher. "Don't point it at anyone. It will just go off and kill them. It has a mind of its own."

Beacher looked it over and finally picked it up. I could tell he got a shock and asked if he felt it.

"Yes," Beacher said. "Never had that happen before except when I scooted my feet on a wool carpet in some girl's bedroom."

I went on to tell him, "This gun will keep you alive, but be very careful and not to let it turn you to its dark side. And never let anyone else pick it up."

Beacher looked it over, and said, "It's about the same gun I been carrying all these years. Does it shoot straight, Sam?"

"Yeah, straighter than any gun I ever owned before."

Beacher just slid his Colt over to me and said, "Okay, I'll trade with you."

"No," I told Beacher, "the gun is a gift. Marie La Veau told me to give it to you; not trade or sell, just give it to you."

With that all said, I just up and left the cantina and Mexico behind me.

*****

Beacher joined Red and Hitch at the bar and ordered a beer. He stuck his old Colt in his belt and Sam's in his holster. Sam's gun was perfect match, except for the scar on the barrel. Beacher was thinking, *'I may start carrying two guns.'*

Hitch asked Beacher, "Is that the Sam Bass that Joe always talked about riding them Indians around tied to a wagon wheel one time up in the nations?"

"Yeah," Beacher said, "the one and only. I know now why Sam Bass scared the heck out of Joe Tolbert. Tell you about it someday."

Sam wasn't gone long enough for Beacher to finish his beer before six or seven banditos rode up to the hitching rail across from the cantina. They stirred up a lot of dust and you really could not tell how many there were; it must have been thirty days past a rain. Only three of them crossed over to the cantina and walked into the middle of the room.

One of them said, "Disparo alhijo de una perra (shoot the son of a buzzard)!"

Beacher had already turned around to watch them. So did Red and Hitch. The outlaws never got their guns all the way out before Beacher shot all three of them by himself. Sam's old Colt just seemed to jump into Beacher's right hand and killed all three of them. He shot the last one before the first one hit the floor. They were all dead before the other Rangers got their guns up. The banditos at the hitching rail saw what happen and left town in a hurry.

Red and Hitch both were staring at Beacher. "Damn," Red said. "Heard you was fast, but don't ever point that gun at me!"

Hitch just stared at Beacher and never said a word.

Beacher never told Red or Hitch about the gun Sam Bass had given him. He was thinking they were better off not knowing about the old Colt. Beacher just reloaded it and they all rode back to Del Rio, Texas. *Let the Federales figure out what happen all by themselves.'*

*****

After crossing back over the river into Texas, I decided to go and see Marie La Veau again. I still could not get over her and dreamed about her all the time. So, I just lit out downriver toward New Orleans.

I final looked at my map and headed more east until I came to greener territory. I was still thirty days from New Orleans had no idea what I was going to do when I got there. "But I got thirty days to figure it out," I told myself.

I rode through swamps and snake infested trees until I was about ready to turn back. I finally came to a sign that said, 'New Orleans, thirty miles.'

I stopped at the first store I came to and bought myself a new black outfit and a bath along with a shave. I got the gray hair from my face and head. Looking in a mirror, I decided I wasn't that old after all. I put my buggy and horse up in a livery and rode my old black horse downtown, looking around for a place to buy. I found what I was looking for on Bourbon Street. A two story red brick building had living quarters upstairs and two big rooms down on the main floor. It was an old building that needed some repair and new window frames. I bought for half the money I had stashed under the buggy floor. I did all the repairs myself, painted a big sign and got it hung over the sidewalk. I had a big black horse painted in the middle of the sign, with the words Black Horse Saloon beneath. Then I went to hiring girls to wait on tables and a big creole woman to cook.

Marie La Veau came around and wanted to set up a card table in the center of the room. She still wore a red dress and a white shawl. It was the beginning of a long friendship. I was still thinking she was a good looking woman.

*****

Poncho Villa was mad as heck when he found out Beacher killed three of his generals. He got so mad he had the ones that escaped with their lives shot by a firing squad. Just stood them up against a wall and shot them. Villa vowed to cross the river himself and kill Beacher, alone. Texas was having growing pains about that time. There was a lot of barbed wire getting strung up and some ranchers feuding between themselves because of it.

Beacher got a wire sent to the sheriff's office. Roho found all the Rangers at Rosa's Cantina after lunch. The wire told Beacher to send Red to Sonora, Texas. *"Wire headquarters when you get there. Send Hitch to Llano with the same orders."* Beacher was to go back to San Antonio, Texas and see Luke Tolbert.

Chapter 4

Unknown to Beacher, about the same time he gunned down three of Poncho Villa's men in a Mexican Cantina with Sam Bass's old Colt 45, Texas Ranger Luke Tolbert had just cleaned up the counterfeiters and burned down their house. Luke had carried all the men to the local funeral parlor in San Antonio, Texas. Being by himself, Luke had used a double barrel sawed of shotgun he borrowed from his friend Sully.

Luke eased up to the basement door where the men were running the press. He just kicked in the door and pulled booth triggers, dropped the shotgun, pulled both of his Colt .45s and shot anything still moving. It was a brutal killing, but it had to be done. Counterfeiters in Texas were hung or shot, no exceptions.

Captain Riley had said there was going to be a Federal Marshal in town sometime next March and this was late February. Luke carried all the outlaws to the coroner's office and told the proprietor, "I will look in my wanted book and see if I could identify any of them." The only one there in his wanted book was a short man, bald head, wire rim glasses, heavy set, scar over left eye, named Speck Littlefield. Littlefield was wanted by the New York state police with a twenty-five hundred dollar reward, dead or alive, for counterfeiting. It got Luke to wondering why a state would pay that much money on a counterfeiter. Then, he remembered some of the 1861 big green-back fives were issued by some cities. If you looked on the back, you would see the city's name that issued them.

The ones Luke had recovered before burning down the house either said New York or Boston. The plates he recovered said New York. Luke hoped the Boston plates were hidden inside one of the walls of the house he'd just burnt down. He got worried about it and sifted through the ashes of the house the next day and found them. They were nearly all melted, but Luke could tell they were the Boston plates. He slept better that night. He had Captain Riley to look the plates over the next morning, then Luke spent the next week in the office filling out paperwork.

The Federal marshal showed up. His name was Liam Johnson. He was a big fellow who looked like a whiskey barrel on stilts. He had long, skinny legs, tight fitting pants, and high heel boots; higher than normal. He had his breeches stuffed down in the boot tops and long, red, curly hair and a handlebar mustache. He had on one of them round top hats with a short brim. Luke believed they were called Bowler hats.

Luke nearly laughed out loud, but held it in. He stuck out his hand. "Luke Tolbert," he said, and they shook hands. About that time, the coroner came into the office said that he'd kept the bodies out of the ground for as long as he could.

Luke had the cemetery worker bury the counterfeiters in the pauper's section with no markers, except for Speck

Littlefield. He had a stone marker made with his name on it, with 'counterfeiter' under it.

"There's a reward to be paid on them engraved printing plates you recovered," said Marshal Johnson. "From New York city and Boston. Five thousand dollars each."

'Now, how I'm I going to collect from New York City?' Luke was thinking,

Johnson said, "I can go down to the bank with you and make out a warrant. The bank will make payment for them and collect from New York and Boston. But we will have to deface them plates to where they can't be fixed and used again. Then, they have to be mailed to a federal Judge in New York City and Boston."

Luke finally got paid on both the outlaw and plates and collected his back Ranger's pay. He transferred all his money to the First National Bank in San Antonio, Texas. The banker, Jim Houston, came up while Luke was there and asked if they could visit. Luke followed him to a desk.

"Luke Tolbert," Houston said, "you got any idea how much money you have on deposit here?"

"No," Luke said.

"Well, let me tell you, Luke. After the money transfer from Fort Worth, as of now, you're one of our biggest depositors."

Luke was not a big spender, never was. He lived on half of his Ranger pay. The only thing he bought in two years in San Antonio were two new .45 Colts, by mail order, a new gun belt with two holsters made on it, twelve new shirts and pants and two new pairs of boots.

The banker wanted Luke to let him loan out some of his money. Houston told Luke that the carpetbaggers from up north were loaning out money at twenty percent. Now, Luke had no idea what he meant.

"You could make a lot of money," Houston told Luke. "And I will stand behind every loan. If they don't pay back the money lent out, the bank will. The bank will just be using your money, and pay you fifty percent of interest we collect."

Now, Jim Houston had gotten over Luke's head about fifty words back, so Luke just said, "Yes, go ahead." It looked like, at the time, Luke had over fifty thousand dollars in Jim Houston's First National Bank of San Antonio, Texas.

This got Luke to thinking about Mary. He sat up past midnight and wrote her a letter. Since she'd invited him to supper one evening before he left Fort Worth for San Antonio, they had been writing back and forth nearly two years. She was John McKenzie's oldest daughter, the sheriff of Fort Worth, Texas. Luke was thinking about asking her to come to San Antonio and visit for a spell.

Chapter 5

Luke made his way to café the next morning and ordered coffee, bacon, eggs and hot cakes. He was hungry. He saw the clerk from courthouse, who came over to Luke's table asked to sit down.

"Sit," Luke said, "and have some breakfast on me."

"Luke, I've got your deed here," the clerk said.

Luke had filed a homestead on close to two thousand acres up and down both sides of the Salado River just north of San Antonio.

"You need to put it in a safe place," the clerk said. "The banks have some safety deposit boxes for rent for a dollar a year. The boxes are in their big walk-in vaults."

"I will do that after breakfast," Luke said. They had our meal and coffee. Luke paid for both meals and they said their goodbyes and Luke thanked the clerk for his help. He walked to bank and saw Jim Houston and asked him about a safe deposit box.

Houston assigned Luke safety deposit box number six and wrote it in a ledger. Then, he asked Luke to sign his name on the line. After he signed his name, Houston handed Luke a key with the number on it, then showed the Ranger to the vault. A lady clerk watched Luke like he was going to rob her, until she saw his badge. Luke placed his deed in the box, along with a pair of old Colt

.36 Army revolvers he had taken the time to clean up and wrap in white butcher paper.

"Are you the Ranger whose been helping out some women here in town?" the clerk asked.

"Yep," was all he said. Luke left the bank and made his way to the post office. He stopped on at a saddle shop and got himself a long leather string. He looped the security box key through it and hung it around his neck. He did not know what else to do with the key.

When he finally got to the post office, Luke fixing to buy stamps when the clerk said, "Luke, you've got a letter from Fort Worth, Texas."

'Well, I better read what Mary has to say before I mail hers,' Luke thought. He went outside and sat on a bench out front. It wasn't Mary's handwriting and Luke had never seen it before. The letter read; "Luke Tolbert, Texas Ranger, San Antonio, Texas. I hate to inform you, but Mary was in a buggy that overturned with a freight wagon. She died at the local doctor's office. The sheriff asked me to write you. The funeral to be as soon as possible."

Luke sat there a long time. It must have been close to noon. He took his time walking to the cantina, Sully's Place, and ordered a cold beer. Luke spent the rest of the day brooding at a back table. Sully came over, sat down and looked at Luke.

"What's wrong, Luke?" Sully finally asked.

Luke told him what happened. Sully never said a word. He just got up and brought two beers with two shots of red eye in them. "Let's get drunk," he said.

Luke had never gotten drunk before and didn't that night. Instead, he just visited with Sully. Luke told him he was going to ask for a transfer to El Paso, Texas.

"Man," Sully said, "that's wild country. A lot of Mexican bandits out there."

That was the last time Luke saw Sully. A Ranger's life was too hard for having a wife anyway. Luke told Captain Riley he was getting tired of San Antonio and asked about El Paso.

"Well, we need a Ranger in El Paso. The Mexican bandits have been robbing banks in El Paso and sneaking across the border," said the captain. "The Rio Grande River there is just a small stream. You can cross it on your knees and not get your backside wet. The sheriff can't cross the river, but a Ranger can. I got papers from the Mexican government that say a Texas Ranger has the same authority as a Mexican Federales does. I'll get you a copy of the papers. When are you leaving?"

"In the morning," Luke said, "after a good breakfast at the café."

"I'll get them papers to you in the morning."

Captain Riley met Luke for breakfast. They had a good meal and a lot of coffee. Luke hoped he remembered how to cook as it had been a while. They said their goodbyes and Luke walked down to Dollins' hardware store. He asked Dollins to improve on his land; to build a fence around it good enough for cattle and a house with four bedrooms, the kitchen with a storage area for garden canning. He remembered his ma having one. He also asked for a porch on front and back big enough to have company on. Luke wanted the front to face east and west with clap board siding and painted white. Luke told Lam see Jim at the First National Bank. "Give him your bill and he will see you get paid," he said. "But try to keep the bill under two thousand dollars."

"I can brick it later if you decided on it," Lam Dollins said. "It won't cost that much."

Luke asked if he had a house in town. "No," Lam said, "I'm just renting for now. I'm planning on building one someday."

The two shook on the deal. While Luke was holding Lam's hand, he said, "Lam, when you get the house finished just move in. Treat it like it was yours."

Lam's wife overheard the men. "Luke, are you sure?" she asked.

"Yes," Luke told her. "I'm going to El Paso today and don't know when I'm coming back, but it would be nice to have a place when I get back. And, Lam, build me a barn and corral if you have time to."

Luke left spent the next hour getting supplies packed on his mule. He left San Antonio riding Boy, leading his mule. He'd just had new shoes put on both. Luke put the papers Riley gave him in his money belt, along with two hundred dollars. He had nearly forty dollars in change in his pocket, some silver and small gold coins. He left another hundred in small gold coins in a leather pouch tied up under his saddle out of sight.

Luke left town riding west. It took him two weeks to get to Junction, Texas. There were a lot of hills, small bushy cedar trees and white rocks. A man couldn't farm it if they wounded to.

Luke figured out why they called it Junction. Six trails converged there. A café, livery barn, trading post and a well were all the town boasted. Luke rested two days. He felt he had gotten soft with too much stable time over the last two years. The man who ran the café said it was close to two hundred miles to Fort Stockton, but there was a new Army post and five streams in the first hundred fifty miles. The last fifty miles were nothing but dessert.

"Well, I never seen a desert," Luke told him. He advised Luke to carry plenty of water after I crossed the fifth creek.

"Don't lose count," the café owner said, "or you and horse could just about starve for water. It gets hot sometimes."

Luke bought extra water canteens and water bag for the horses and filled them before he left Junction.

*****

Billy Bours had worked as a lumper on a steamship line up and down the Mississippi River for nearly ten years before he saved enough money to buy a freight wagon and a team of mules. He bought them off an older man who had a Studebaker wagon and four young mules. It cost Billy nearly all his savings. He gave the old man fifty dollars per mule, and one hundred twenty-five for the wagon. He had enough left for supplies and road money.

Billy had acquired a freight contract with the Union Army, to move freight from a steamship dock in Memphis to Army forts out west. The first load he moved was to Fort Stockton, on west of Fort Worth, Texas. He'd never been there, but the steamship had very good hand-drawn maps of Texas, Arkansas and Indian Territory.

Texas was a lot bigger than Billy realized. It had to be close to an eight hundred mile trip at thirty-five cents per mile. He bought insurance from the freight office for a penny per mile, which cost him eight dollars. The trip would pay two hundred and eighty dollars with the commanding officer at the fort paying on delivery. They never put a timeline on a delivery for early trips west. It was new country, most of it, and impossible to set a timeline on how long the first trip to Fort Stockton would take.

Billy just walked his mules and let them water as long as they wanted to in every creek and river crossing he came to. He had a water barrel, but always tried to kept it full. It took him close to a month to get to Junction, Texas. He bought some oats and fresh hay because he'd already fed up what he bought for the trip. He still had about two hundred miles left to Fort Stockton.

The days had gotten a lot warmer. Billy was sitting on the wagon seat, just ambling along, and about half asleep. It was just about midday when four Mexican banditos and one peon riding west to Sonora, stopped under the shade of a large cactus to lunch on some beans and tortillas they had stolen at Junction, Texas.

They saw a wagon and mules coming toward them, with the mules just walking along and a man on seat asleep. They could hear the driver snoring above the noise of the wagon wheels on the gravel trail. The peon got up and let his donkey go. He ran and jumped on the wagon step, then jumped into the seat and pushed the driver off onto the ground.

Billy did not wake up until he hit the ground. All he saw was his wagon going on west without him and a Mexican peon in the seat, dressed in dirty white cotton clothes and a big brimmed hat. Billy could not run fast enough to catch them and wore himself out. He knew where Junction was, but he had no idea how far it was on to Sonora.

Billy turned around and started walking back towards Junction, Texas. He walked for two days getting back to the last river he crossed.

Chapter 6

Luke never made it to Fort Stockton. About a day and half after riding west of Junction and crossing the Liano River, Luke stopped to let Boy and his mule water for as long as they wanted to. He knew this was the last river between here and Stockton, with nearly fifty miles of desert looking on west. Luke was sitting on Boy, looking at the countryside. Heat waves on west made the scenery disappear. He wondered about it somewhat. He knew the heat caused a person to see things you knew were there.

Luke saw a man walking, then he just disappeared. He looked at spot for a while and the man reappeared, getting bigger. A trail of dust was following him. The man was dragging his feet. Luke could not tell if he was a Mexican or a Mescalero Apache. With the heat waves rising above him, sometimes he was visible and other times he wasn't.

Luke pulled his Colt out and kept it in his lap, an old habit. The man was getting bigger all the time. It took him close to an hour to reach the spot by the Liano River where Luke sat. The man never paid any attention to Luke, he just walked up to bank, threw his hat on the ground and fell in the river. He stayed there in the water, soaked and splashed around and drank water for what seemed to Luke was close to an hour. He finally climbed out and sat on the riverbank. He sat there rubbing his eyes, soaked his old hat in water and put it on. Only then did the man take a close look at Luke.

The man then said, "Some Mexicans pulled a gun on me. Five of them stole my freight wagon and mules. The damn thing is loaded with long guns, shells, food and Army uniforms that was headed to Fort Stockton. I need to get to the law. Can I borrow your mule?" It was about that time that Billy saw Luke's badge. "Ranger, I'm glad to see you. It happened near two days ago. They headed on west. There's not a lot of wagons on the road this time of year, which make it easy to track them down."

Luke saw that the man was what was known as a bull whacker; they all wear them rabbit ear boots, meaning they have long leather pulls on each side made them easier to pull on.

Luke sat there pondering what to do. He could not leave the man afoot and it was too far back to Junction and him with no water bag. Luke had one, but his horse and mule would need it.

"What's your name?" Luke asked.

"Billy Bours," he said.

"Luke Tolbert," the Ranger introduced himself and stuck out his hand. "Well, Billy, help me move thing around on my pack mule."

It took the two men an hour to get things moved to where Billy could ride. He sat on pack saddle with

Luke's bedroll under him. It would have to do until they could find a horse.

The two tracked Billy's wagon all the way to Sonora, Texas, a nice little Mexican town, where the wagon tracks turned south to Del Rio, Texas on the border. Ciudad Acuna, Mexico was just across the Rio Grande River. It was getting dark, so they stayed in Sonora that night and slept in the jail.

The next morning, they were at the cantina having breakfast when Billy whispered, "Luke, that's one of them bandits." He pointed with his fork at a short greasy-looking man with two guns on.

"Let's just watch him until he leaves," Luke told Billy. "There's no need killing other folks in a crossfire."

As soon as the Mexican left the cantina, Luke and Billy left also, but not too close. He was just about to mount his horse and Billy and Luke were about fifty feet away from him.

"Hold up there," Luke called out. "The law needs to talk with you." At the sound of Luke's voice, the Mexican went for a gun. Luke shot him dead center. The Mexican bandit flew back nearly six feet, dead. Luke looked in his Ranger's wanted handbook, but there was no paper on the man.

Sheriff Joe Walsh came up. "Is that one of them banditos?" he asked.

"Yep," Luke answered. "You seen him before?"

Walsh studied the dead man for a while. "No, I got nothing on him."

"Well, get your people to bury him," said Luke. "Anything in his pockets and his guns is yours. Me and Billy are taking his horse. Any objections?"

"No," replied Walsh.

Luke and Billy set out for Del Rio, Texas. "How many mules did you have pulling your wagon?" Luke asked.

"Four," Billy said. "The load is very heavy so they can't go very fast. It's not much better than a good walk. They've got nearly four days head start on us."

Watching the tracks, there was not another wagon on the road. Just some saddle horses. The wagon tracks were deep, so it had to be Billy's rig. They came to a river and stopped to let horses drink. It looked as if the road followed the river for a ways. Luke took out his Texas map. The river was called Dry Devil and went all the way to Del Rio before it dumped into the Rio Grande west of the town.

Riding on south alongside of the river, there was heavy grass spot under some live oak trees. They almost missed where the wagon tracks left the road and went into the river. Billy said they may have been getting the wheels wet to keep the iron rims from getting too loose and coming off. They never came out of water, just went on downstream. Billy and Luke must have followed it ten miles or more. There was a lot of grass along the bank and it was getting dark. They made camp and had plenty of food as Luke had packed for El Paso. It was warmer this far south, but Luke was not complaining.

They never saw the where wagon came out of the river until the road crossed it again.

"Damn," Billy said, and stopped in the road. He got down, studying the tracks. "That wagon is empty. How in the hell could that have happened?"

Luke and Billy studied on it a while. The supplies were not in the river or they would have seen them. The bandits must have built a raft and unloaded the wagon and rafted the supplies downstream, figuring if the driver caught up with the wagon, he would not know where supplies were. The man driving the wagon could then just say he'd found it empty.

Luke looked at his map. The Dry Devil River dumped into Rio Grande nearly ten miles west of Del Rio. "Billy," he said, "the only thing we can do now is follow your wagon."

So, they headed south. The bandits must have been running them mules. They was throwing chunks of dirt behind their tracks. It looked like they ran them all the way to Del Rio.

Luke and Billy arrived in town late, close to dark, and found a livery stable to put up our horses. Luke made a deal with the proprietor to let them sleep in the loft over their horses. Then, they found a café.

"You got any money?" Luke asked Billy.

"Some," he replied.

"If your money gets short let me know, okay?" said Luke, then ordered their meal.

Billy did not have a gun. Luke made a mental note to see he had one. Two or three guns was always better than one. After their meal, they made their way to cantina. There were several in town to choose from.

The bartender spied Luke's badge and said, "Them damn Mexicans across the river come over here, robbing and stealing, and just ride back across the river. The sheriff can't follow them. Even you Rangers can't follow them and put a stop to it."

"Now we can," Luke said. "I've got a paper from Mexico City allowing Rangers to cross with the same authority as the Mexican Federales." Luke then ordered a cold beer for himself and Billy. "You got any guns and holsters you've taken off them Mexicans?" Luke asked the bartender quietly.

"Yeah," the barman replied. "I've got two and a good holster made of heavy cow hide." He laid them on bar. One was an old Remington Navy, rusty as hell. The other gun was a Colt .45 with nearly all the bluing gone. It looked like Luke's. He put his finger on the .45.

"How much with holster?" he asked.

"I don't know if it shoots or not," said the bartender. "How about a dollar?"

Luke laid a silver dollar on the bar. The barman picked it up and put the old Navy back under his bar. Luke looked at Billy. "You ever carry one?" he asked, pointing at the gun.

"Yes," he said, "in the War Between the States."

"It's yours," Luke told him.

Billy belted it on. "Thanks," he said. "I'm going to shoot that damn Mexican for running my mules when we catch him."

Chapter 7

Luke and Billy Looked around Del Rio until noon and covered the whole town. The sheriff saw them prowling around and wanted to know what their business was. Luke showed his badge.

"Name's Sam Watson, Sheriff of Del Rio," he introduced himself.

"Luke Tolbert, Ranger. My pard here is Billy Bours, a bull whacker. Mexican bandits took his freight wagon just west of Junction. He was headed to Fort Stockton with freight for the Army post. It was loaded with guns, shells and Army uniforms. We tracked it south of Sonora and seen the place where they drove the wagon into the river. We followed it nearly ten miles downstream where the road crossed the river and picked up the tracks again. It looked like the wagon was empty. The tracks were not very deep, so we reasoned they were rafting the freight downriver. The wagon we tracked into town was empty."

"Dry Devil is running a lot of water," Watson said. "It would take them three or more days to reach the Rio Grande. That old Dry Devil is as crocked as a dog's hind leg. From where the road crosses north of here, there're not any docks on the Mexican side of the Rio Grande. They would have to unload on the Del Rio side. The only dock around is just south of town."

"Damn, that's good news," said Luke.

"Why?" asked the sheriff.

"That means the wagon has to be in town," said Luke. "They will have to load the wagon from the dock and then cross the Rio Grande with the loaded wagon. It's the only way to get freight into Mexico."

They spent rest of the day searching, but found no wagon or mules.

"Billy, let's spend rest of day looking them cantinas over," Luke suggested. "We may come across one of your Mexican bandits. If I remember right, you said the one driving, when they took it from you, was a peon, wearing all white with a big hat on. He's got to still be in town."

They searched over six cantinas before Billy found him, maybe. He was sitting at a table, drinking clear tequila, all by himself. He had no hat on and it looked like he was going to have a long night.

Luke and Billy crossed the street and sat on bench in front of another cantina and waited on the Mexican to leave. They had begun to think the peon was going to spend the night when, around midnight, he came staggering out. They followed him to edge of town to an old adobe house. The house had one wall gone. It was a real dark night with no moon.

"Well," Luke told Billy, "let's go and get our horses and be here before daybreak. We can hide our horses in that wash between the adobe house and the river. He will have to come our way going to the docks." They found a real low spot where all the Mexican could have seen was their hats.

At sunrise, they watched as the mules and wagon were brought out of the adobe. The place was not that big. The Mexican must not have unhitched the mules or watered them all night, because as soon as they smelled water, they broke and ran all the way to the river. They ran right out into the water until they were belly deep, then stopped and went to drinking. That Mexican peon was just hanging on for the ride.

Luke and Billy rode up beside him. Luke hollered out, "You're under arrest!" The peon saw Luke's badge, jumped into the river, and began trying to swim. It was too deep to run in and not deep enough to swim in, so he was just splashing around, making a lot of noise. It was kind of comical to watch.

Billy rode up next to him and pulled the old Colt .45 out. BOOM! "That'll teach you to run my mules," he said, then spat tobacco juice at him as he was floating downstream.

Billy let his mules drink their fill. He walked his team in the water for nearly an hour, letting them do what they wanted to, then finally said, "I need to take them into town and get them some oats and fresh hay."

"Okay," said Luke. "I will watch for the raft. Hold up a bit, Billy." Luke rode up to wagon. "Billy, when you get your mules taken care of, see if you can find me a double barrel shotgun, a sawed off one."

"I got one under the seat," said Billy, "if them Mexican bandits haven't found it." Billy looked under his seat. It still there; a big double barrel ten gage loaded with double 00 buckshot.

Luke thought it looked like Sully's old gun. "How come you didn't pull it out when them Mexicans came at you, Billy?"

"Well, hell, Luke I was asleep," Billy told him. "It was a hot day and I was napping under my hat. I didn't even wake up until that damn Mexican pushed mc out of the seat and I hit the ground. All I seen was them driving my mules and wagon off."

"Billy," Luke said, "bring me some food from one of them cantinas." He gave him some change. "I will hide down by the dock and wait on them to float downstream."

Luke hid Boy in a draw not too far from the dock. It must have stuck out fifty feet into the river. He found a place on the downside of the river to hide. Luke did not like to get wet and stayed that way for a long time. He waited on them there. Luke wondered more than once if he was in a bad place. He pondered on it a while and decided that there had to be two men on the raft. It would be too hard for one man to control. Then, another man would meet them there and wait for the wagon to show up. Luke got up and started walking back to Boy's hideout. He felt hiding place was too out in the open and he would be seen by someone coming on horseback.

A Mexican bandit came out of a draw right in front of Luke, saw his badge and went for his gun. Luke out drew him, and hit his horse in the head. It stumbled. The bandit's shot missed. Luke fired another round almost point blank into him. He hit the ground in front of Luke, dead. Luke looked to see if the raft was coming.

"Now what?" Luke said aloud. "Those two on the raft will see their partner piled up here and make a break for it." So, Luke pulled the man over to the river and rolled him in. Downstream he went. Luke got Boy and used the Mexican's rope to pull his horse into a draw, hiding him. He picked the bandit's old rusty gun up and threw it into the river with him.

About an hour passed before Billy showed up. He saw the dead horse in a draw and Luke told him what happened.

"Only two left," Billy said.

They sat on the dock and had supper, which wasn't bad. Luke was thinking again. "Bill, let's tie the horse you're riding up to the dock. It's one of theirs and they will think the other bandits are here. It belongs to one of them anyway." Once Billy got it done, Luke said, "Now, you hide and I will just sit here on this dock with that big hat on from the one I shot. It's getting dark and if they show, they will think I'm asleep."

Luke must have nearly beat that old hat to pieces before he got all the fleas out of it. About one past midnight, the full moon was out. Luke could see a raft in the moonlight. Sure enough, two men with poles were pushing it to his side of the river, Luke had a poncho over his shoulders and the shotgun in his lap, both hammers cocked back. He pretended he was asleep. Luke waited until they got the raft tied up to the dock, then threw the poncho over his shoulder.

"You boys are under arrest," Luke said. Both of them went for their guns. They were only fifteen feet apart. Luke already had some experience with the big double tens. Boom! He pulled both triggers same time. When the smoke cleared, those boys were floating downstream, face down, dead.

"Billy," Luke said, "go get your team and wagon. I will help you load it up."

Chapter 8

Luke saw Billy on the road back to Sonora, Texas. They said their goodbyes. Billy handed Luke that double barrel ten gage and said, "You got me this Colt and I never pulled the trigger on this old gun. I'm kind of scared of it anyway. It would be a good trade for you." He handed Luke the shotgun and a box of ten gage shells, which Luke stored in his saddle bags.

Luke told Billy, "Just tie that old horse on the back of your wagon. You may need him again someday."

Luke stayed in Del Rio two days. He'd seen they had a telegraph office, with wire on poles clear to Austin, Texas. He sent a wire to headquarters and told them what had happened with a government shipment of guns and supplies going to Fort Stockton. He also told them he'd recovered the stolen guns and supplies in Del Rio. Luke let headquarters know that if he was still needed in El Paso, he'd head west up the Rio Grande.

Luke hung around town waiting for an answer. When he got a wire back, it said the local sheriff had caught the bank robber. Turned out, it was the local banker, an inside job. The sheriff caught him trying to sneak out of town on the stage to Van Horn. The sheriff had seen the banker get a ticket at the stage office and wondered why. The lawman watched him load up. The banker had no large bags, just one little bag. When the sheriff made him open it, it was full of money. The townsfolk were trying to hang him. The wire said the sheriff just might let them, because his own money in the bag, too.

The wire from headquarters said they were having trouble over to the east in a place called Uvalde. Some outlaws were robbing people on the stage line between Uvalde and Eagle Pass. *'Go down the river to Eagle Pass. It's a lot better traveling than straight east to Uvalde.'*

The next morning, Luke headed out to Eagle Pass. He was needing a bath. The soft living in San Antonio had gotten to him. His shirt was about worn out. Luke had new one in his saddle bag. When he saw a good spot in the river, he decided there was still too much daylight left. He did not want someone sneaking up on him with no gun on.

Luke camped real close to the river that night. He found an overhang and built a fire back in a cave. He was nearly out of sight. Before the moon came out, he got his bar of soap and headed to the river. In no time, Luke had bubbles going downriver. He got out by the fire and dried off. He felt a lot better, and slept until coyotes woke him up. Luke liked to listing to them howl.

When the moon comes out, a man can see near as good as daylight if his campfire is out. It had always been Luke's favorite time of night. He was lying there awake when he saw ripples on the water. An Indian was trying to sneak up on Luke. He was alone and Luke thought he must be a Comanche or a Mexican. It was hard to tell at night. He could not see any clothing. His saddle bags were next to him, so Luke got out his spy glasses. No one was visible on other side of the river, so Luke figured the Indian had to be alone.

Luke reached over got his yellow boy, laid it across his pack saddle, and aimed at the Indian's head. He must have been around two hundred feet out in the river, making straight for Luke's camp. The water wasn't two feet deep all the way across the Rio Grande. If he wasn't sneaking, he could have walked to Luke's camp.

Luke shot the Indian, heard a loud 'whap,' and saw him floating on top of the water. Downstream he went. White man, Indian or Mexican, it didn't matter to Ranger Luke Tolbert. If they sneaked into his camp at night, they were going to die. Luke strapped on his guns, took his rifle and glass, and made his way to the top of the bluff. He stayed behind some brush for nearly an hour. There wasn't anyone around on either side of the river. It quiet rest of the night; the coyotes were even quiet.

The next morning, Luke rode into Normandy. There was just a little cantina right on the bank of the Rio Grande. He had some steak and eggs with plenty of coffee. There was a big old oak tree out front. The cantina just had three walls and was open on the side next to the boardwalk, looking toward the river. It was a real nice place.

Luke hid his badge. He didn't want people to know a Ranger was in the area. He overheard some people talking about finding a dead Indian on a snag at the river's edge, shot in the head. Luke thought it must have been the one that tried to sneak up on him the night before.

Just ambling along, Luke arrived in Eagle Pass at noon. Since he was not in a hurry, he didn't go straight to the sheriff's office. Luke wanted to meet the lawman on the street. That way, nobody would know he was a Ranger.

Luke started checking out cantinas. Some of them looked pretty rough. Most of the patrons were a mix of Texans and Mexican cowboys. He ordered a beer from the bartender.

Luke spent the next four days doing the same thing- watching to see who was spending more than a normal cowboy. He found himself guessing they were either all cowboys or outlaws. It was hard to tell the difference.

Ranger Tolbert finally saw the sheriff. Luke was setting in the shade outside a cantina after his noon meal over with. He saw the lawman look his way and was sure he'd been watching. Luke pointed to empty spot on the bench. The sheriff came over.

"Sit," Luke told the sheriff.

"Maybe I don't want to," answered the sheriff.

Luke opened his lapel so the sheriff could see his Ranger badge. The lawman sat down.

"My name's Windle Homes," he said. "I'm the sheriff here about."

"Luke Tolbert, Texas Ranger."

"Heard of you," Homes said. "I've been watching you, wondering who you was."

"Headquarters sent me down," Luke replied. "You got any idea who's doing all the robbing from here to Uvalde?"

"No" the sheriff replied, "and I haven't seen any big spenders around either. It's got me stumped. Hell, I know just about everyone around here. There are not many strangers in town, that's why I was watching you."

"Are there many big ranchers around?" Luke asked.

"Yeah, one," said Homes. "Whistling Hough Minor has his spread up north and east on the Nueces River. Real nice spread close to a place called Montell."

"Why do they call him Whistling?" asked Luke, curiosity getting the best of him. "That can't be a Christian given name."

"He got that name because anytime he rides a horse, he whistles," said Sheriff Homes.

"Just how big is his ranch?" asked Luke.

"Near thirty thousand acres or more," replied the sheriff. "It's an old land grant from Spain. Texas agreed to recognize them when we kicked them Mexicans south of the Rio Grande."

"Think I will ride up towards Uvalde in morning," said Luke, "and look around."

There were six roads leading out of town. It was no wonder the sheriff was having a hard time catching any outlaws. Luke saw a lot of mountains to north and west on his way to Uvalde. He left his horse and mule at the livery.

The man at livery saw Luke's badge. "Keep it to yourself, can you?" asked the Ranger.

"Yeah, maybe until Saturday night," the livery man said.

"What's Saturday night got to do with it?" asked Luke.

"I always get drunk" the man told him. "Then I can't keep my mouth shut."

Luke was hoping maybe he could catch the outlaws before Saturday night. Being late, he went straight to the sheriff's office. The street quiet. When Luke walked in, the sheriff was doing paperwork on some wanted posters. A new list had just come into his office. Luke never said a word, just pulled up a chair to his desk got out his Ranger handbook and updated it. The sheriff stopped and watched Luke. When he got finished, he stuck out his hand.

"Roho Gonzales, Sheriff," the lawman said.

"Luke Tolbert, Ranger.

"I've heard of you," Gonzales said.

Now, that was twice in the same day that someone had said they'd heard of the Ranger. It made Luke wonder what the hell everyone knew. He did not like being in the dark. "What have you heard about me?" he asked Gonzales.

"Wagoner, a rancher up north, was telling Minor, a big rancher north of here, about you beating him out of his big black horse and five hundred dollars," the sheriff related. "He said you hit a playing card at fifty feet, just pointed your gun, pulled the trigger and hit it dead center. Is that a true story?"

"Yep," Luke said. "Hard to believe he came back. The horse is out front. Take a look if you want to. The horse still is not branded. Hell, WT Wagoner might get a chance to win him back some day. No need marking him up."

Roho showed Luke a rooming house and livery barn. The rooming house had meals and a bath. Luke thought he stick around for a while, but then again, he might ride up to Montell and see what kind of person this Whistling Hough Minor was.

Chapter 9

Luke Stayed in Uvalde until Friday before deciding there were no big spenders around. He decided to ride up to Montell and look Hough Minor up. He rode north in the morning, nearly twenty five miles to Montell. It was not much of a town, just a hardware, bar, a bank, livery, one hotel, a church and a café. There was no sheriff's office, so Luke stopped at the café. The horse trough was empty. Luke saw a bucket well in the middle of the street, so he pulled up the bucket and got water for his horse and mule plus a little extra.

Just as Luke walked up to the batwing doors of the saloon, a rider came up and tied his horse to the hitch rail and started inside. Luke stopped him and pointed to the near empty water trough. The little buzzard swung at Luke. Luke did not want to kill him, so he ducked under his swing and kicked his feet out from under him. Down he went. Luke kicked him out into the street, told him when he got up to water his horse.

An older man and woman rode up about that time. "Son, what's going on here?" asked the man.

"That man kicked me."

"What for?" he asked.

Luke spoke up. "I told him to water his horse and the trough is empty."

The older man saw Luke's badge about that time. "What's your name?" he asked.

"Luke Tolbert, Texas Ranger."

The older man said, "Todd, you stay out here and fill that trough up full."

"Yes, sir," was all he said.

The older man stepped up on the porch. "My name's Minor. This is my daughter, Sara. The boy out there is Todd."

They all went inside. Luke found a table and was fixing to sit down.

"Mind if we join you?" Minor asked.

"Sure, have a seat," Luke said. When Sara got out of her riding duster, hat and gloves, Luke decided she was about the best looking woman he had ever seen. She was not too tall, slim waisted, with a better than average build.

They ordered their meal. Luke had steak, bread, fried potatoes and peas, something he hadn't seen since leaving home.

Sara could not take her eyes off Luke. Minor asked the reason Luke was in his part of country.

"There's been some outlaw gang robbing the stage and travelers between Uvalde and Eagle Pass," Luke explained. "I was not having any luck finding them, so I decided to spread out some."

"You the one that beat Wagoner out of a black horse and five hundred dollars?" Hough asked.

"Yes," Luke said, being in a woman's company, "the black horse is tied out front."

Sara said, "I bet you spent that money real fast."

"No," Luke told her. "It's in the First National Bank in San Antonio, Texas, drawing interest."

She said, "Interest? What's that?"

Luke spent the next hour trying to explain it, with Hough Minor laughing all the time.

Todd was still not talking to Luke because he was still mad.

"Where are you staying?" Hough Minor asked.

"I haven't made up my mind," Luke replied.

"Well, the hotel here is a flea nest," said Minor. "Come out to my place. Make it your headquarters while you're in the country. We've got a lot of extra rooms and would enjoy your company."

Hough Minor gave Luke a room upstairs, across from Todd. Sara's was down the hall. In the next two weeks, Luke must have ridden two hundred miles and talked to every cowboy in the country. He even rode the stage back and forth between Uvalde and Del Rio. It seemed the robbing had stopped.

Luke wired Austin and said the outlaws must have moved on because the hold ups stopped near a week before he arrived, with none since his arrival.

Luke hung around for answer. He got a wire back telling him to stay another two weeks. If the robbing had stopped, he was ride to Hondo. There was a land dispute going on down there.

Luke spent the next three weeks with Sara, riding on her father's ranch and looking at cattle. He found out a lot about cows that he never knew before. Those old longhorns were very mean, old bulls mainly. Luke decided being a cowboy was not for him.

At one point, he felt like telling Sara about Mary, but changed his mind. Some things were better left alone. The two got to sparking around some, but nothing serious. Luke tried to get her to go skinny dipping with him, but she was afraid some of the cowboys would see her, or her dad. Sara said he would just shoot first and talk later, so they decided against it.

Luke told Sara he had to leave the next day for Hondo, something about a land dispute between some ranchers. Sara came right out and said, "I will ride with you. I need to visit my aunt in San Antonio."

Luke helped her pack nearly all her things in her buggy the next morning and tied Boy, along with his mule, on the back.

Hough had been watching them. He came out and said, "You taking her off, are you? It's about time she settled down. She's fixing to be seventeen years old; you know?"

"No, Pa," Sara said. "I'm going to visit Maggie in San Antonio."

"Then you're coming back?"

"Yes, Pa," she replied. With that, the two left for Hondo.

Luke and Sara drove east across the Minor ranch to Sabina. It was a small town with a flea bag hotel and livery. The hoister saw Luke's badge.

"I'll take care of yours and the lady's horses and buggy," the hoister said.

"Keep it inside," Luke told him. "And it better all be there in the morning."

"Don't worry," said the hoister, "I'll watch it close."

Luke got a room for each of them. It was just about dark when they went to the café. The food was not bad. After they ate, Sara said she was tired and was going to lie down. Luke sat on the boardwalk for a spell, then turned in also.

They made Hondo by midafternoon, had lunch and rested Sara's horse in the shade by a water trough. Carrying fresh water, Sara said she could make San

Antonio before dark. She had made the trip many times before, she told Luke.

"You sure you will be all right?" Luke asked her.

Sara showed Luke a shotgun under the seat, and said, "And I know how to shoot it."

Luke told her if she needed anything to go see Jim Houston at the First National Bank and tell him Luke Tolbert sent her.

Sara gave Luke a kiss. He watched her leave and went looking for the sheriff. He walked to the livery to see about Boy and his mule. Luke was still looking for the sheriff. He found the jail but there was no one there. He sat on a bench out front, watching cowboys. There were a lot of tied down guns, not normal for ranch hands, so Luke decided to hide his badge for a while and kind of feel things out.

Finally, Luke decided he needed to move. He walked to the local cantina and ordered a beer. The barkeep set it in front of Luke. After he was paid and before he could turn away, Luke asked him who was the sheriff in Hondo.

"Joe Walsh, why?"

"I was just wondering," Luke told him. "I seen a lot of riders with tied down guns."

"There's a range war fixing to happen," he said.

"Who's the ranchers involved?" asked Luke.

"Well, there's Tom Horton southwest of here," said the bartender. "His headquarter is in Frio. And then, Harvey Pearsall over east in a town named after him. Horton is claiming all the water in Frio River. He says he has and old land grant form Spain, but the filing dates don't match in Mexico City with the record books and Texas won't recognize it. Old Horton won't let Pearsall's cattle water in the Frio."

Luke decided to ride south. The Frio and Hondo River fork on his map showed a small, natural lake there. Luke was thinking that if there was a range war fixing to happen, it was over either grass or water because, in this part of Texas, both were in short supply. The only thing there was not a shortage of was Mexicans riding small mouse-colored horses and longhorn cattle.

Luke camped next to a large pond on the river that he thought must be the Frio. He built a fire under some big old oak tree that would be nice cover for the early morning fog. While he was fixing breakfast of bacon and coffee, he saw a group of riders coming, faster than normal. They were in a hell of a hurry. Luke sat on his saddle next to the campfire, shotgun cocked, cross-legged, with the sawed off ten gauge Billy gave him in trade for that old Colt Luke had bought for a dollar.

Luke had the Colt in his lap, pointed their way. He sat there drinking coffee, when one of the men yelled "Disparo al hijo de una perra!" Luke knew enough Spanish to understand the words meant, "Shoot the gringo!" He pulled both barrels of the shotgun at the same time and rolled off his saddle to his knees. He pulled both .45s and shot anything that was still moving. Luke killed two horses and three Mexicans.

One was gut-shot, so Luke asked him, "Cuyo rancho Es esto? (whose ranch is this)" Tom Horton was all the man said before he died. Luke knew his headquarters was in Frio. He took a page from his handbook and wrote, "Don't send gun hands after a Texas Ranger." He then laid note on dead Mexican with a rock on top of it.

Luke left the dead men there and rode to Frio, Texas. It was a small place on the bank of the Frio River with a cantina, livery barn and café. To Luke, it looked like a lot of other places in Texas.

He stopped at Rosa's Cantina asked the bartender for a beer. Luke was drinking real slow, watching everyone in the room. He took a table in the corner and sat there until his belly was growling. Then, he walked over to the café.

A little Mexican woman asked, "What will you have?"

Luke told her, "Filetey and Huevos." The waitress, Juanita, brought Luke steak and eggs. From where he sat, everyone in the room was visible. The cafe opened onto a veranda. The back wall had a fireplace in the middle of the room, and the east and west walls opened onto a boardwalk. Luke had just paid his bill when a young boy came running a horse up the road. The horse had dried blood on it. It wasn't long before twenty-five riders were following him back down the Frio River road.

Luke needed to go see Harvey Pearsall and find out what the hell was going on. He rode south of Frio nearly ten miles before heading east to Pearsall. He found the livery and took the time to hide his badge. Luke asked the livery man where he could find Harvey Pearsall.

"Well, Harvey's been hiring gun hands," he said. "His headquarters is east of town, five miles on down the Hondo River."

Luke found a barber shop and spent five cents for a shave, hair trim and a bath.

Chapter 10

Luke had breakfast before leaving Pearsall for Harvey's place, but he still got there before noon. The main house sat on a rise, higher than the corrals or bunkhouse. It was surrounded by oak trees. The house and walls had never been painted. It was an old Spanish mission adobe-style and kind of looked like the Alamo. It even had a wall nearly six feet tall all around it and a large wooden gate that was open.

Luke rode in. There were horses in the corral, but no cattle in sight. Some cowboys were breaking wild stock. He counted ten men, all sitting on the rail, watching a tall skinny fellow ride a bronco until the horse just wanted to stand. The cowboy poked him with his spurs and made him walk around the corral. Luke rode on up to the main house where three men were setting on the porch. The tie rail was under some large oak trees nearly a hundred feet out from the porch.

There was a large old well with a bucket rope under its roof. The horse trough was full of water. Luke left Boy there and walked to the steps of the porch. He stopped on the bottom; it was never a good idea to go up steps uninvited.

"Is Harvey Pearsall here?" Luke asked.

"That would be me," an older man answered. "Who's asking?"

"Luke Tolbert."

Harvey got up and walked to edge of the steps. He stood there a moment and then said, "Boys, meet the man that outshot W T Wagoner for five hundred dollars and that big black horse tied up under them trees. Come on up and have a seat."

Luke and Harvey shook hands, then Harvey introduced the two men as Jack and Earl. After their handshake, Harvey said, "I thought you was a Ranger."

"I still am," Luke replied, and showed his badge.

"Have a seat and visit a while," Harvey said. "What brings you this far south? I heard you was fixed in San Antonio."

"I was until I found out who I was looking for," Luke replied. "I burnt their house down."

"Damn," both boys said. "Why?"

Luke spent all evening tell that story.

*****

Sara arrived in San Antonio late in the day near dark. She was driving her buggy up Main Street, just past the courthouse, when two kids jumped on her buggy from a boardwalk and grabbed her purse. It was just a small bag with a draw string around top, but they took off with it and all the money she had with her. She was madder than a wet hen. The two boys they ran up an alley and were gone. With no money for a room or supper, she just went on to Maggie's place and got there after dark.

Lam Dollins was loading up his wagon up with furniture. Sara asked, "Lam. what are you doing, leaving town?"

"No, just moving to a new home."

Maggie heard her voice. "Sara, is that you?"

"Yes."

"Girl, you're just in time to help us move." Sara told Maggie about getting robbed by two children. "Oh, my. What is going on in this town?"

Luke had told Sara that if she needed anything, she was to go see Jim Houston at the First National Bank. Sara did just that the next morning.

"I'm Sara Minor," she told Houston. "My father is Hough Minor."

"I know him," Jim said.

Sara told the banker about getting robbed by the two children. "Luke Tolbert told me if I needed anything, I was to see you."

"Why sure," replied Houston. "How much money would you need for your stay in town?"

"Not much twenty dollars maybe," said Sara.

"No problem," Houston assured her. "Why don't I advance you fifty dollars, and if you run short, just let me know."

Sara told him she was staying with the Dollins family.

"I know them," said the banker. "Lam is building a new house for Luke Tolbert."

"The Ranger?" Sara asked.

"The one and only," Houston said with a chuckle.

"How," Sara asked, "can a Ranger afford a new house?"

"How well do you know Luke?" Jim asked.

"Well, he stayed with us a spell," Sara told him. "He used our place for a headquarters some."

"Well," Jim Houston explained, "not many people know it, and don't spread it around, but Luke is one of the richest men in San Antonio."

Sara left the bank feeling lightheaded. She drove her buggy on to the hardware store. Maggie joined her and said, "Give me a ride out to our new place."

A fence started just at the edge of town, three wires with split rail posts. "Just under two thousand acres," Maggie said. "It belongs to a friend of ours. Lam built a new home with four bedrooms, kitchen, dining and living room, with a fireplace and an inside bathroom."

"What is an inside bathroom?" Sara asked.

"You've got to see this," Maggie said, and showed it to Sara. "It has a water closet up on the wall," Maggie explained. "When you pull the handle, water flows down to a bowel and makes it flush. And, there's a metal bathtub."

"Now, that is something I've never seen before," said Sara.

"Lam built a windmill and water tank about head high out back of the house," Maggie said. "That's where the water comes from."

Maggie and Lam talked Sara into staying with them for the rest of the summer. She was going to talk her father into one of these new bathrooms as soon as she got back home. Maggie cautioned her not to tell anybody about the bathroom until Lam got one built at the hardware store to show people. Maggie said every woman in town would want to come out the house to use it.

*****

After Luke visited with Pearsall better part of the day, he learned the war was over an old land grant. The way Harvey described it; it was pretty much like the bartender had told Luke. It looked like a false claim. Several Mexican families had tried to falsely clam land grants. Harvey's lawyer had looked into the dates of the filling and was sure it was a false claim. The dates did not match up with dates in Spain.

Tom Horton claimed the Frio River on both sides down to the fork, with the Hondo River and on south for two miles along Hondo. It left Pearsall without any water most of the year unless it rained. A lot of times, just the lake was the only water for miles.

Harvey had taken steps and moved his stock south nearly twenty miles on the Frio and Hondo Rivers where there was a little water in the river. Then, moving them on south as water dried up and hoping for a rain. Harvey was hiring men for a war with Horton.

Harvey said, "I know it's coming because Horton's men were shooting at my drovers any time they crossed paths. It's just a matter of time until they will kill some of my men and the war will be on."

"Well, I think your war just started," Luke said, and told Harvey about his encounter with some riders at the Frio and Hondo pond. Luke also told Harvey about the note he left on one of the men. "I rode on to Frio and was going to confront Horton, but I never got to," Luke continued. "He rode out of town with twenty men or more, headed south down the Frio. If he was coming here, he would have showed up by now."

Harvey scratched his beard. "He won't show in daylight. That sneaky skunk will try to come in the dark and burn me out of this old house. It was claimed as his headquarters in the Frio land grant. Horton swore he would see it burn to the ground if he could not have it. He may come tonight, maybe not. Who knows?"

"How many riders do you have here at ranch?" Luke asked.

"Counting my two boys, twelve not counting me and the cook," said Harvey.

"Well, count me in," Luke told him. "They already made a try for me."

So, the watch started that night and went on for nearly a week before any Horton's men were spotted. They were easy to spot, as they were all Mexicans on mouse brown short horses.

All of Harvey's men were armed with them Yellow Boy .44/40s. They were a pretty good gun, if you took care not to drop it or let your horse lean again a post. The brass was easy to bend and it would jam up a lot. Sometimes you could straighten them out, if not, it made a good wall hanger.

Luke and four other men took to sleeping in the daylight and staying up all night. Just as the moon crept out one evening, they spotted a group of men. There must have been around six of them creeping up on the main house. Luke and the other four cut loose on them at a hundred feet. The intruders were out in the open. Luke didn't think they got off shot before they were all down. Walking around, Luke and Harvey's men found their horses, stripped them of their guns, tied them in the saddles, led them past the Frio pond and spooked the horses. Luke fired several shots behind horses, figuring they would run all the way to Frio Luke had taken the time to put a note in each dead man's pocket that just said, "Texas Ranger."

The same thing happened a week later. Luke was beginning to think Horton couldn't read English, so this time, he wrote the notes in Spanish. Luke was beginning to think this was the dumbest bunch he had ever come across. As suddenly as it began, they just stopped and everything calmed down. Luke thought maybe Horton was getting short of Mexicans.

Chapter 11

A week later, Harvey's boys, Jack and Earl, were in town. Some Mexican cowboys, probably some of Horton's hands, jumped them, beating them black and blue all over. Some of Harvey's cowboys brought them home in a wagon. Harvey Pearsall was mad as hell and told Luke he was going to end this tomorrow.

"What you got in mind?" Luke asked.

Harvey sat there a while, then said, "I have a case of nitroglycerin in the cellar that's still got the cotton packing around it."

Luke said, "I've have heard it's hard to move without blowing yourself up."

Harvey said, "I know how."

Harvey gathered himself some old clothes and boots, some with them with the long straps on each side, and with a big hat, Luke thought he looked like Billy. Then, he went outside told some hired hands, "Go get me that old Studebaker wagon with a pair of mules hitched to it." Harvey then walked out to the barn and built himself a big box out of lumber that had extra nails and a canvas waterproofed tarp.

Harvey drove the wagon out to cellar, nailed the box in the middle of the wagon floor, then put the tarp in the bottom and over sides. He eased the case of nitro upstairs and sat it down inside of the wooden box. Then, he filled it with water and placed a big rock on top to hold it down. Harvey explained that water made it stable. He got a white rock and drew an x on both sides of the wagon box in line with nitro.

"There's your target, Ranger," he said. Then, Harvey got up in the seat and took off for Frio. "Don't follow me too close, Luke. You need to sneak into Frio and stay way behind me."

Harvey looked like a mule skinner with some freight, just taking his time. They arrived in Frio just after dark. Harvey parked his wagon under that old oak tree out in front of Juanita's café. The cantina was next door. He unhitched his team and led them away. Nobody paid him any attention. Luke met up with Harvey under some trees at the edge of Frio.

"Now what?" Luke asked.

"Can you see the x on the wagon?" asked Harvey.

"Yes," Luke replied.

"Think you can hit it with one shot?"

"No problem from here," said Luke. "It's not over three hundred feet. Easy target."

"Well," said Harvey, "let's just wait. Them boys and old Horton always stop at Juanita's every night for Tequila. And, they always tie there horses up under that old oak tree out front. Horton will be with a bunch of Mexicans."

The two waited nearly an hour before Horton showed up. "That's him," Harvey whispered in Luke's ear.

Luke had taken up a spot with a fork in some trees that made a good shooting rest. From where he was, the mark on wagon box looked to be around two hundred feet from his rest. He knew he could not miss. Just as Horton walked past the wagon, Luke pulled the trigger on his .44/40.

Luke's hat flew off, Juanita's roof left her café, sand and dirt stung his face, and he was sure his ears would ring until the next day. Every leaf on that old oak was gone. They were still raining down as Luke and Harvey rode of.

The explosion killed ten Mexican bandits and Horton. The only thing left of the wagon was the wheels. Every other piece of it was gone. Luke meant to ask if they heard a big bang all the way in Austin. Nobody in Frio ever knew what happened and nobody saw Luke or Harvey as they just rode out of town real slow.

The next day Luke picked two splinters out of his face. The war was over.

Luke wired Austin a short note. It read: "Luke Tolbert, land despute over. No one left alive to calm old Spanish land grant." He got orders back the next day; "Some trouble in San Antonio. Get there ASAP." Back to

San Antonio ASAP got Luke's attention and he wondered what was going on.

Luke left Pearsall early before sunup. There was nice, damp air early on, but he figured it was going to be hotter than hell close to noon. He must have been close to seventy miles north to San Antonio. Luke made good time until noon, then slowed Boy to a walk. He stopped at Rossville, Texas, at a little cantina that had shade trees and a well. Luke filled up the water trough and let Boy and his mule drink their fill. He loosened the saddle's belly strap.

The cantina looked a lot like the one in Frio before the roof flew off. Luke ordered steak and eggs, then asked the waitress if she had folks in Frio. Luke was just having a friendly conversation, when a rough looking cowboy came in. He walked behind the waitress and booted her with the flat side of his boot. Tears came to her eyes.

The cowboy said, "I told you not to be so friendly with every cowboy that comes in here." Then, he turned and went to the bar. Luke heard him order a shot of Red Eye and a beer.

Now, Luke didn't see this as a situation that required killing, but it did call for an attitude adjustment. So, he just walked up behind the cowboy and kicked him as hard as he could, lifting him up in the air. He came down, broke his nose on the bar and melted into the floor. The cowboy looked like a pile of rags lying there. Luke made sure everyone in there saw his badge.

"He had it coming," said the bartender, and went on about his business.

The cowboy laid there until Luke finished his meal. As he began to move around some, Luke walked out, tightened up Boy's saddle strap and left town.

He got to San Antonio at dark and went to livery stable. Bud was there. They said their greetings, then Bud took Boy and Luke's mule. Luke grabbed his saddle bags and walked to the boarding house. He was lucky to get a room that late in day.

Luke was up early the next morning and had breakfast on the porch. Then, he walked to Ranger headquarters.

Captain Riley said, "I'm glad you're here. We've got some people passing some counterfeit bills, different than others."

They were all 1862 bills, the same big five dollar note. The one Riley showed Luke was a lot different than the 1861s. Luke looked at the 1862. "What's wrong with it?" he asked.

"Well, the '62s have a red seal stamped at the first stamping," said Riley, "then, they're stamped with signatures of the Secretary of the State. The writing will be on top of the red seal, not under it. The counterfeit bills have red seal stamped last and all the writing is under the seal."

"What makes you think they're printing them in town?" asked Luke.

"Well, this was the first place the banks found any," Riley answered.

"Ok," Luke said, "I will visit with Jim at the First National and see what I can find out."

When Luke got to the bank it was near lunch time. He saw Jim and suggested they eat and visit some. The first thing Jim wanted to talk about was Luke's money.

"Luke," Jim Houston said, "I made you a deal to loan out your money and split the interest. It sounded good to me at the time, but I forgot about operating expenses, building upkeep, labor, taxes, and everyday expenses like paper, ink and so on. All the money you made was all profit and I paid expenses. That was my mistake. You're way ahead of me in the bank profits. Heck, your account of deposit is over a hundred and fifty thousand dollars and mine is just over sixty thousand. According to the bank auditors, you're the owner of this bank."

The two men ordered lunch and finished their meal before Luke said anything. "Jim, you're a good friend," Luke said. "I'm back in town to catch some new counterfeiters. I will not take over your bank, and I don't ever intend to. Let's just go on like we were and let me pick up my share of the operation expenses. From now on, all I need is an office desk where I can come and go long enough to catch these new counterfeiters."

"Okay, Luke," Jim agreed. "Sounds good to me. What about a title?"

"What do you mean, Jim?"

"Luke, you need a title just to keep them state auditors happy," Jim said. "How about Vice President?"

"Well, I never was Vice President of anything before," Luke chuckled. "Jim, I need a house in town where I can watch for them counterfeiters."

"I've got just the place for you," Jim said. "Let's go for a walk."

Two streets north of the bank on cobble stone street with oak trees on both sides, the houses were all Colonial style. They were big homes, red brick, cobble stone driveways, and all of them two story. Luke counted eight total.

One on the north side, in the middle of the block, was a two story of light brown brick. A white picket fence ran along the street and around the house. It had red clay tiles on the roof, white painted windows, and a big porch must have been fifty feet wide and fifteen deep. The white posts, four of them, were large enough that Luke could not reach around them. It had a stable of to one side and, around back, a large fenced in area.

Luke and Jim went inside. The house was completely furnished; rugs on the floors, stuffed chairs, drapes on every window, beds all made up with pillows in every room. There was a big table and eight chairs in the kitchen with a big cast iron stove.

Jim said, "Everything goes with the sale. The old woman said sell it for five thousand five hundred dollars and wire her the money to New York City. She was going back home."

Luke spent the next hour looking the house over. There were four bedrooms upstairs, a large living area, fireplace and kitchen. "When can I move in, Jim?" he asked.

"Now if you want to," Jim told him.

"Okay, I'll take it."

The two men walked back to the bank. Luke noticed a street sign on a post that said Cherry Street. He turned around and saw 1028 on the porch steps of the house he'd just bought. Luke asked Jim if he needed to sign papers on the deal.

Jim said, "We can take care of it later. Say, you need to go see Dollins. Man has he got a surprise for you."

"What?" Luke asked.

"Well now, it won't be a surprise if I tell you."

Luke picked up Boy at the stable and retrieved his saddle bag from the boarding house. Then, he rode to Dollins' Hardware. Maggie saw Luke coming up the street and told Lam.

Dollins met Luke on the boardwalk. "Luke," he said, "I got your house finished and a little extra. Let me show you."

Lam took Luke to the back of his store. He opened a door and said, "You ever seen a bathroom inside?"

"No," Luke told him. "I never heard the word before."

Lam showed Luke a water closet up on the wall, head high, with a large pipe going down to a bowl bolted to the floor.

"Pull that rope," Dollins said.

Luke pulled it and water rushed into the bowl and everything went down. "Where did it go?" he asked.

"Outside to a tank in the ground," said Lam. "It has pipes with holes in them about two feet deep and a hundred feet long with a lot of rock around them. The water just goes away." The bathroom even had a bathtub with a drain and a mirror on the wall with a wash bowel under it.

"Dollins," Luke said, "I have got to have one of these."

"Well, I took the liberty of building you one in your new house," said Lam.

Maggie was watching the two men. "Luke," Maggie said, "we can move out soon as we find us a place."

Luke said, "We need to talk about that, Maggie. You and Lam just stay where you're at. There's no need for you to move, now or ever. I just bought me a place in town at 1028 Cherry Street."

"Man," Dollins said, "that's a nice house."

Luke asked Dollins, "Can you put two of these bathrooms in for me? One upstairs and one down? With running water in the kitchen?"

"When?" Dollins asked.

"Start today if you can," Luke told him. "I already bought the house." Luke saw Maggie wiping her eyes. He walked past her and said, "Good friends are hard to come by."

She grabbed Luke in a bear hug, said thank you, and kissed him on the cheek.

Luke said, "Maggie, can I ride out to your place and use your bathroom? I can't wait to try one out."

"Go ahead, Luke. We will be home near dark and fix supper."

Chapter 12

Luke rode out to the house Dollins built. He did a good job, Luke was thinking. It had a nice fence, the house was painted white with two long, low covered porches that had four posts on each one. There was a windmill out back with a large tank made of wood about head high, with pipes going into the back of house. There was also a small livery barn about a hundred feet north of the back porch.

Luke put up Boy and went inside. He carried his saddle bags with him, which had clean clothes packed in them. He looked around and saw all the bedrooms. Two of them were being used. *"Well,"* he thought, *"happens sometimes. Couples sleep in different rooms. Maybe Lam snores."*

Luke found the bathroom. He looked it over. Luke got the water turned on in the tub and found a plug for the drain. He laid out his clean clothes, then found some soap. He piled his dirty clothes in the floor. Luke was standing there in his birthday suit and never heard the door open.

All at once, a woman screaming. Luke turned around and Sara was standing there. She stopped screaming and just stared at him.

"Finally," said Luke. "What are you doing here?"

"Well, I was in a state of shock," said Sara.

"What are you doing here?" Luke repeated.

"Maggie is my aunt and I've been staying with her this summer," Sara said.

Luke didn't know why, but he found himself blurting out, "Well, you can either stand there and watch, or you can just join me."

Sara turned, closed the door and locked it.

It was after dark, when the Dollins got home. Luke and Sara were fixing supper. Sara had brought home some fresh beef and bread from town.

Maggie was staring at Sara. She knew something was up. Luke was frying steaks and Sara was cutting up some potatoes to fry, making every opportunity to touch Luke. Maggie finally said, "What the hell is going on here? Sara, how long have you known Luke?"

"About an hour," Sara said with a devilish grim.

Luke jumped in and told Maggie, "We met at her father's place nearly two years ago. I used his place for a headquarters for a while, then rode with her when she was coming to San Antonio. I had no idea she was still in town, let alone out here. I only realized she was here when I went in to take a bath." Luke's face flushed and he closed his mouth. He knew he'd already said too much.

Maggie was still staring at Sara. "And I suppose you had a bath, too, Sara?"

Sara just whispered, "Yes."

Before he realized it, Luke hurriedly said, "We're fixing to get married, tomorrow."

Maggie asked, "Does Sara know you just bought a new house?"

"No," Luke said, "it's a surprise."

"Well," Maggie said, "I'm her aunt and Hough Minor's sister. He will not miss your wedding."

So there it was. It had taken Luke only four hours to make Vice President of the First National Bank of San Antonio, buy one of the biggest homes in San Antonio, use a bathroom in a house for the first time, get in bed with the best looking girl in town, and get married. That was faster than a shootout with a gang of outlaws.

Maggie said, "You need to let Hough know when to be here."

Sara was standing there with her mouth open. "Where did you buy a house?" she asked. "Some parts of this town's not fit to live in."

Maggie told her, "I will show you tomorrow. Luke is going to be busy buying a suit." Maggie just stared at Luke.

"Yes, ma'am," was all he said.

"And get a rider to go out to Hough's place or ride out there yourself," Maggie added. Lam was laughing so hard he almost made himself sick.

After supper and the lights went out, Sara was sneaking into Luke's room. The bed broke down, making a lot of noise, and the two of them laid there waiting on Maggie to show up. Thankfully, she never did.

Luke and Sara got up before daylight and fixed breakfast. He told Sara he was going to ride out to the ranch and ask her father for permission to marry her. Luke kissed her goodbye, something he'd never before.

It took Luke the better part of the day to get there. Hough Minor was sitting on porch, drinking coffee, when he rode up. Luke took the time to water Boy, then asked about putting him in a stable and a small amount of oats. They'd had a long ride today and had another one tomorrow.

"Sure," Hough said, and told Todd to see after Luke's horse. Todd seemed to be in better mood than last time Luke had seen him.

They sat on porch and talked a while before Luke finally got around to the subject of Sara.

"You seen her?" Hough asked.

"Yeah, I have," said Luke, "and we decided to get married, if it's alright with you"

Hough said, "It's taken you long enough. She's be gone near two years. Can you make her a living?"

"Well, I own two homes in San Antonio, one just north of town on the Salado River with near two thousand acres under a three wire fence. Lam and Maggie Dollins are living there. The other one is at 1028 Cherry Street, two blocks north of the First National Bank that I'm Vice President of."

Hough looked at me and said, "Held the damn thing up, did you?"

"No, Hough, I just been very lucky and worked my tail off when I was very young," Luke said. It took him two hours, telling Hough about his years in Illinois, the reward money and his deal with the banker, Jim Houston.

"You about ready to settle down then?" Hough asked.

"Yeah," said Luke, "I been thinking I would just stick with banking and hang up my badge."

"Okay," Hough said. "So, when is the wedding?"

"As soon as we get back to town."

Maggie drove Sara in her buggy that morning down to Cherry Street. When they turned on the street, Maggie stopped and sat there looking around. "Sara, are you sure we heard the address correct?"

"Yes, I wrote it down," said Sara. "I did not want to forget." She got out her note; 1028 Cherry Street.

Maggie started on down the street and they finally saw house numbers down by steps. When they came to 1028, Maggie stopped in middle of street and sat there a while, afraid to go in. Dollins rode up in his wagon about that time and just pulled up next to the porch and went inside. The women followed him.

Maggie said, "Lam, are you sure about this house?"

"Yes," he answered, "I saw Jim down at the bank. This house and everything inside of it belongs to Luke Tolbert."

"Everything?" Sara asked.

"Yes," Lam said everything. "Now, Sara, where do you want to have the bathrooms? Luke said one downstairs and one up, with running water in the kitchen."

Lam was looking outside at the water supply. Most of the houses just had a bucket well, but this house already had a windmill. All he needed was a water tank up high enough for water to flow into the home.

Sara and Maggie had found some chalk in Lam's wagon and were marking out walls for the bathroom. Lam could tell they had already changed their minds twice, they had chalk marks all over the floor.

Lam decided he better step in then. The bathrooms had to be on outside walls. The one downstairs needed a door to the bedroom and access to the living room.

"Why?" the women wanted to know.

"Heck," Lam said, "you want company going through your bedroom just to get to the bathroom, do you?"

"Well no," both women said.

"Okay," Lam said, "we need two doors then."

Lam went out to the wagon and got a long rough-sawed two by four near ten feet long. He laid it down and drew chalk lines on floor. He got the rooms laid out and the women finally agreed. Lam said, "Go shopping, you two. I got a crew coming."

Before the day was over, all Lam liked was wallpaper He'd let the women take care of that.

Luke and Hough, along with Todd, made it back the next day. Luke was thinking he'd be glad when the wedding was over with so things could get back to normal. That was ironic, for he was Luke Tolbert, Texas Ranger, and things never got back to normal.

The End